The text of this book is set in Georgia.

The illustrations are pencil.

Ohmstede, Catherine Sauls.

Sugar Witch / by Catherine Sauls Ohmstede, MD

Illustrated by Mary Draper Hager

Summary: Fictional tale of a magical girl who learns the value of healthy eating.

ISBN 9798352136935

Sugar Witch

By Catherine Sauls Ohmstede, MD

Illustrated by Mary Draper Hager

To our fathers, who taught us to treasure art and health.

And to Eleanor and Henry, who made it happen.

There lived a girl in a faraway world who ate nothing, but candy.

It tasted good. She called it food!
She always kept it handy.

Her black cat named Lolly kept her jolly as she sat eating all day in her room.

With candy canes, or sours, she passed the hours, too full to fly her lollipop broom.

Every morning she ate chocolate.

At night she enjoyed treats.

Her teeth fell out! There is no doubt,
one cannot live on sweets.

"What shall I do?" the sweet girl cried, a lollipop in each hand.

"Sweets are nice, but I paid the price! Now I can hardly stand!"

One day she found out, without a doubt, her candy supply was completely dry!

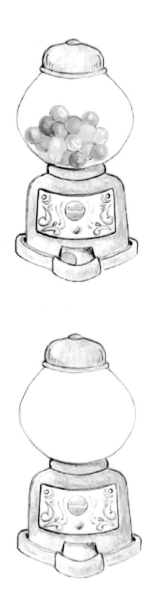

She needed to find more food. She put on her hat, picked up her cat, and mounted her lollipop broom.

She tried to fly, but my, oh my, too weak to fly was she. She fell to the ground and looked all around, but saw no sweets, or treats.

To her surprise, something green caught her eye.

She took a bite. To her delight,
broccoli tasted... all right!

She started eating fruits and veggies
each day and each night!

Each day as she flew, she saw her strength grew. One day she realized, to her surprise, she found happiness through good food and exercise!

She hatched up a plan, lollipop broomstick in hand. She did what she knew that she should.

She took out paper and pen and wrote down her plan to send to children worldwide.

"I will share a healthy life's joys with sweet girls and boys by turning their candy into toys!"

To the children she wrote: "In October hang my picture in sight. Leave your candy outside on Halloween Night. In its place I'll leave something better! A book, skates, a toy, or a sweater! In the morning instead of candy, you'll find a gift that's good and dandy!"

With fewer sweets to eat, children will have cleaner teeth. They will find joy resides with good food and exercise.

For it is true: sweets are not good for you. They may taste great, but you need on your plate good food and time outside if you want to fly.

During the month of October, children around the world hang a picture of the Sugar Witch in the front window of their homes so she will know to select a gift for them to receive on Halloween Night.

Follow these steps to draw your own picture of the Sugar Witch to hang in the front window of your home next October!

1. Draw two circles in the middle of the page for eyes:

2. Draw 2 circles inside of the circles:

3. Fill in the big circles, leaving the small circles blank:

4. Draw an oval with a flat bottom around the eyes and a small U-shaped mouth between the eyes:

5. Draw an upside-down U shape at the top of the head:

6. Draw 2 diagonal lines down from the bottom of the head:

7. Connect the lines with a wavy line:

8. Draw 2 long U-shaped arms:

9. Draw a U around her head and connect the bottom to her dress:

10.Draw a long U for each leg:

11.Draw her lollipop broom:

12.If you want, you can give her a witch's hat:

13. Color your picture and hang it in the front window for all the world to see!

Catherine Ohmstede, MD is a pediatrician and mother of two delightfully sweet children in Charlotte, NC. The Sugar Witch visits her home every Halloween Night.

Mary Draper Hager is an artist and beloved 2nd grade teacher in Charlotte, NC. She inspires her students by surrounding them with creativity, art and beauty.

Made in the USA
Coppell, TX
13 October 2022